Praise for Eden Winters

Diversion is one of the strongest gay romance novels I have read... It maintains a perfect balance between romantic comedy and hot sexual tension on the one hand and a solid, fascinating, complex plot about prescription drug smuggling on the other...

—Val, ARe Cafe

Forget sleep, I had to find out how this worked out. With a fast paced and tense external plot plus a relationship moving to a new level, Collusion kept me turning the page until I got to the end. Diversion, the first Bo and Lucky book, did the same thing to me, and this is a more than worthy followup.

—Crysselle, Reviews by Jessewave

So many things go on in [Collusion]. Some good (Bo and Lucky), some bad (Lucky in the children's cancer ward), but there's never a dull moment. Some smiley, happy ones (Lucky's confrontation with the neighbor from hell), some tear-jerking ones (the cancer ward), but you *need* to know what's going to happen. The story pulls you along to the ultimate, beautiful conclusion.

—Mrs. Condit Reviews

I find myself hesitating, not wanting to put the limitations of a label on such a unique and revelatory series and cast of characters. I only know that I want and need more of them and the dubious path that Winters has laid out before them. It's an amazing journey and I know you will want to be here with me every step of the way.

—Scattered Thoughts and Rogue Words

# THE SENTINEL

## EDEN WINTERS

ROCKY RIDGE BOOKS

Warning

This book contains adult language and themes, including graphic descriptions of sexual acts which some may find offensive. It is intended for mature readers only, of legal age to possess such material in their area.

This is a work of fiction. Any resemblance to actual people, places, or events is purely coincidental.

The Sentinel
©2013 by Eden Winters
Cover Art by P.D. Singer

ISBN: 978-1-62622-023-2

All rights reserved. No part of this book may be reproduced without written permission of the author, except as brief quotations as in the case of reviews.
Second edition, December 2013, Rocky Ridge Books
First published as part of Goodreads M/M Romance Group's Love Has No Boundaries.

Published by:
Rocky Ridge Books
PO Box 6992
Broomfield, CO 80021
http://RockyRidgeBooks.com

For readers who cheer on lonely souls, hoping they'll find their happy ever after.

# CHAPTER ONE

*Move out, but avoid the caves,* the commander warned, the communication resonating through the soldier's frontal lobe implants. *They're lined with crystals that block our signals.*

Soldier Fourteen nodded, snapping the last section of his body armor into place. Prickles raced across his skin, tiny filaments piercing his epidermis, digging in deep to meld suit to body. Properly geared, he joined his brothers on the field. Simple orders today, eradicate the colonists who refused the Federation's demands. Laser fire peppered the air, mixed with screams and pleading. The acrid scent of burned flesh seared his nostrils, but Fourteen ignored the cries of the rebels with their primitive weapons, carrying out his orders with single-minded determination—capture able-bodied youths and destroy any others. His implanted com-link shrieked a steady stream of banter into his mind: officers' instructions, his brothers-in-arms' triumphant shouts as they lay waste to the colonists. Stupid colonists, withholding rightful due.

Through the villages they swarmed, skirting the caves to maintain signal. *Beep, beep, beep, beep!* An alarm shrilled in his ears. He ducked and rolled. Fire blazed through his side. Curled on the ground, he lay perfectly still. A scream and the high-pitched whine of a particle discharge spoke of another soldier's shot in his defense. Take that, you rebel!

Covered for the moment, Fourteen requested, *Damage?*

*Primitive projectile weapon,* came the diagnosis from his suit. *Point of entry: C7 and C8 joints.* Over his left ribs, then, in the vulnerable area between armored plates that allowed flexible movement. A very lucky shot for the rebel. Topical lesions. *Exit point C15 and C16 joints,* the diagnostic program continued. *Circuitry damage in section...* The coordinates streaming through his visor stuttered and went out. Fourteen raised his weapon, but his robed assailant ducked into the cave. Fuck that! Signal or no signal, he'd go in. No one shot him and got away.

Fourteen struggled to his feet. *Diagnostic!*

*Communications circuits malfunctioning,* the tinny voice of the suit transponder replied. *Attempting repairs, maintain position.*

Oh, hell no! Not until he took out the bastard who'd clipped him. Even as he watched, the scratch on his skin sealed and the suit mended itself back together. He shuffled past the mouth of the cave. Silence. For the first time since his parents dropped him off at the Federation recruitment camp, no voices rang in his head, no orders overrode his own thought processes. Only eerie silence.

He'd thought his own thoughts once, back before they'd shoved a com-link into his head, hooked him into a processor, and relieved him of that responsibility. Back then he'd had a family, a name... Fourteen slammed the door on the memory, a memory he'd believed scrubbed from his mind forever. Must be the crystalline interference his CO spoke of.

A series of electric impulses throbbed through his connection with his armor. Yes, though it didn't possess

## The Sentinel

a brain of its own, his suit calmly reminded him that he wasn't alone and probably never would be—not for long, anyway. The sharp bite of a medical filament on his left glute followed, delivering medication and promising sweet relief. The pain vanished; adrenaline leveling out, his heart rate normalizing, and tension melting away. Bless the Federation and their miracle drugs, delivered in perfect doses for each situation. The suit/soldier units proved well-nigh impervious: he'd seen near-corpses continue battling. Drugs, circuitry, programming, and nothing to lose made for one hell of a soldier.

Sweeping one arm back and forth while seeking a target with unaided vision, he probed his now pain-free injured side with his fingers before venturing farther into the cave. *Engage sensors,* he intoned, wondering how much the suit had managed to repair itself. A stream of numbers filled his periphery, faded and incomplete in some cases: temperature, Federation time. Life forms. An infrared beam emitted from his visor. There! Weapon! The suit selected a tight-beam laser—useful in confined spaces with possible ricochet factor. The tingling at his fingertips told him *armed and ready.* Making use of the shadows, he advanced on a huddled form on the floor, the tips of his mitt aimed and ready to fire. But first, what did the enemy look like, the foolish one who'd defy the government?

Two life form signatures appeared in his vision feed, one weak, one strong. He eased forward, ready to duck if necessary. A thin river of red seeped from beneath a gauzily wrapped form. A rebel? Without armor? What was this flimsy garment the thing wore?

A pale face stared up at him, lips moving, making incomprehensible sounds. He tapped into his com's translator and waited while the program shifted through the being's garbled speech. "Mercy," he finally heard.

And, "Please." The light in the creature's eyes faded, its last breath wasted on a final "Please."

Mission completed, Fourteen checked his side again, preparing to leave the cave. Wait! What about the second signal? Maybe this thing was only a decoy. He searched the body, finding a sling strapped across its front.

Weapon at the ready, he commanded, *Analyze.*

The schematic in his peripheral whizzed through several species and subspecies, finally settling on, *Humanoid, female, infant.*

Huh? He'd been commanded to kill. He poked at the squirming pink bundle wrapped in more of the gauzy material. Didn't look very dangerous to him.

*Danger?* he asked, staring at the mewling creature. So tiny. A long-suppressed memory surfaced of himself as a human, before he'd become a soldier, and his mother presenting him with a similar bundle, named "Sister."

*Helpless,* the dispassionate mind connection advised. Helpless? The government sent a fully charged destroyer at a helpless target? What threat did she present?

Fourteen focused on the wispy covering of the larger creature. Perhaps the older being presented the danger. *Analyze,* he ordered again.

*Humanoid, female, deceased.*

Fourteen peered through his visor for a better look. In the past twenty years he'd battled many of the Federation's enemies, but where lay the threat in colonists? Federation citizens? With only close-range projectile weapons, why engage them at all? Why not rain fire from beyond the atmosphere? Oh yeah, bodies to swell the ranks of the Federation's military, in order to conquer more worlds. Can't spoil the goods.

Images flashed through his mind: his parents screaming, his mother pleading, and then, finally, sobbing and clutching her bloody nose as his father led

# The Sentinel

him out the door, the last time he'd ever seen her. Is that what happened here? Had the older female been told to give up the younger? Is that why the colonists fought? All for naught. What the Federation couldn't get they'd destroy.

Tiny noises escaped the tiny human. Fourteen reached out a hand—why, he didn't know. The infant wrapped miniature fingers around his glove. Then she peered up at him, in all his hideous, bloodied glory... and smiled. "Sister" had smiled, too.

Fourteen stopped, waiting for directives. Nothing. For the past twenty years, the constant stream of instructions had rendered no need to make major decisions. Now, in the calm of the cave, with only his own heart for guidance, he raised his weapon to follow his original orders.

That smile. That guileless smile.

He lowered his hand. Before, each target had offered its own reward: freeing the Universe from anarchists, or repelling marauding invaders. Ending their lives spared his, and the lives of fellow soldiers. But killing harmless colonists? On an agricultural world?

He powered down. Mindlessly cutting a swath through armed and screaming invading forces was one thing, killing a helpless infant another entirely. But what to do? If he simply left the creature in the cave, could it care for itself? Probably not.

The diminutive female smiled again while pulling his finger to her mouth. Hungry. Fourteen recalled a time when he'd put food in his mouth to nourish his body, long before being assigned an enhancement suit to see to his needs and keep him ever ready to fight.

Something in his chest tightened. He'd been young and helpless once.

*"Please, Father, not again!" he shrieked, while his mother stared down at her hands twisted in her lap.*

*Spittle flew from his father's mouth, his nose mere inches from Fourteen's. "You'll do as I say, and you will please the senator. If I hear one bad word..."*

There'd always been a senator, a judge, a magistrate—even a governor. None came to Fourteen's aid. At night they'd taken pleasure from his body, and in the morning they'd opened their doors and surrendered him back to the man who'd continued to use him in a bid for power and influence.

He couldn't turn back time and stop the madness for himself, or for "Sister", wherever she was now. He'd stop it for this child. The first thing he needed to do was get her someplace safe.

His life pod wouldn't make it very far, being designed only for short trips to a planet's surface and back to the ship, but hadn't he heard of another colony nearby? In the midst of battle chaos, pods launching and landing, and interrupted signals, surely he had time enough to hide the child off-world without being missed.

Boom! Dust and rock rained down. He threw himself to the ground and shielded his intended victim with his body until the danger passed. The ground stopped shaking, and his visor adjusted its lens to allow vision through dust clouds. Now or never. He scooped the child from the dead female's arms and tucked it inside his armor, catching a whiff of something clean-smelling. The infant made a warm lump against his chest. A few filaments broke free of his flesh to wrap around the child, cradling but not entering her skin. His peripheral now displayed two heartbeats and monitored two sets of vital signs. He left a gap in the suit so he could peer inside and keep watch over his new charge. Warmth seeped through his skin where she lay.

"You be quiet now, little one," he said in a voice long unused, after two failed attempts to communicate via his implanted com unit. Right. Sergeant would hear via com once he left the cave. Voice only from here on out. Voice. Did he even remember how to use spoken words, or did his voice emerge as primitive grunts?

Trained to stand tall and depend on his suit for protection, now he slunk in the shadows to the mouth of the cave. *Report!* blared through his now active com-link.

*My pack took a hit, intermittent signal,* he replied, grateful that the link only picked up his thoughts and not the yawn from the sleepy child. He stared in horror. The thing had no teeth! How could it eat? Time enough to worry about the future when they survived... if they survived.

*Regroup east of the city,* his commander replied. East of the city. Far from the pods. Fourteen could work with that, and if discovered, could blame his malfunctioning com. But something more must have malfunctioned. He'd been conditioned, fed drugs, had circuits wired into him to guarantee obedience, and yet here he was, no longer under the shield of the crystal-infested caves, making his own decisions. All instincts screamed, Run!

He paused a moment. What could he do for the child's dead mother? With no other course of action, he merely promised, "Your child will live in my care," and set off toward the pods.

Once inside he closed the lid while tucking the infant into a more comfortable position for a long cryosleep. He set course for the nearest colony, then gave himself over to chemically induced slumber.

*Skreek, skreek, skreek!*

What?! Fourteen jerked from sleep and stilled his breathing, straining his brain cells for his commander's voice to explain the claxon. The soft touch of his pod's consciousness greeted him instead.

*Landing in five, four, three, two...*

He'd barely had time to register a stirring beneath his breastplate before impact. Fourteen willed his body limp and rode out the juddering as the pod landed and slid along a soft surface before coming to a stop.

*Damaged circuits twelve, seventeen, thirty-eight, forty-nine...* the pod's connection recited, telling Fourteen what he'd already known. This mad dash to wherever he was had been a one-way trip. Oh yes, Q-218. Colonized.

*Atmosphere?* he demanded.

His peripheral display scrolled complete numbers this time, having had time for repairs: temperature, oxygen mix, not that he couldn't breathe other gases, thanks to his enhanced physiology and a semi-sentient suit, but he'd found the child in a predominantly oxygen atmosphere.

*Nitrogen, oxygen...* More elements ran through his display, the ratios sufficient to support human life.

Satisfied that they'd both survive the air, he popped the entrance on the pod and crawled out into a blinding mix of sand and sun. Sand. Great for landing, but being in the middle of a desert didn't bode well for finding civilization. What? Damp sand? Shells? In a desert? He breathed deeply of salt and seaweed, with no water in sight.

Wherever they were, the child needed civilization. Food, clothing, lodging, and someone who knew how to care for the young.

*Skreek, skreek, skreek!*

Oh, fuck! The claxon. Even now it sent out a beacon, summoning the mother ship to a downed pod. For better or worse, no turning back now.

Parts of him didn't seem to be working, having not yet slung off cryosleep. He dragged himself along on the sand using his heavily armored forearms, his numb legs

## The Sentinel

trailing behind. Surely the damage wasn't permanent. No time for a diagnostic now. How the hell was the child inside his suit still sleeping?

He eyed the pod. Yeah, he should be far enough away by now. He raised his shields, took a deep breath, and held his arm out in front of him, depending on the suit to choose the weapon. *Sorry old friend,* he sent as a mental message to his transport. A single blast obliterated the pod. Nice. Those enhancements he'd gotten on NG-38 had paid off.

Next, he breached his armor, baring his forearm to the harsh warmth of the sun. The little one slept on. He slipped his fingers beneath the plated joint at his elbow, grabbed the faux skin covering, and pulled, revealing a panel mounted deep in the amalgamation of flesh and nanotechnology. *You and I, we go together, little one.* He jabbed a digit into the bright red reset button, forever severing his link with his last commander. Ah, free will. What a wonderful thing.

Scrolling numbers, a mute cry, warmth against his chest. Oblivion.

Scrolling numbers, a shadow blocking the sun. Guttural language.

*Translate!* Fourteen commanded his suit. Mahogany skin and tight ebony ringlets clinging to a rounded head declared the being standing above him humanoid, even without the suit's assessment.

*Old Earth dialect, modified,* the com-link replied, adding, "I am Connell."

The name drifted down into Fourteen's programming, taking hold. *Soldier Fourteen, at your service, Colonel.* The man's face scrunched up into a look the com identified as confusion. Oh, the colonel wasn't wearing armor, and therefore wasn't connected to a com-link. Using his rusty voice, Fourteen stated, "I am Fourteen and yours to command, Colonel." A squirming against his chest, a whimpering cry, and then oblivion once more.

# CHAPTER TWO

Connell stared down into the bay at a bright object flashing in the sun. A gouged track in the sand marked the transport's passing, and for the love of the colony, would someone please make it shut up!

Several times before, Federation pods had landed on New Wailea, and after a ship's beam flashed down from the heavens Connell had helped to fish bits of flesh and hardware out from inside. Strange creatures, half man, half machine, but this was the first time he'd seen one crawl from the pod and struggle across the sand. The Federation could easily obliterate all evidence of whoever earned their ire, and Connell tired of their grisly little reminders of what happened to those who didn't bow to the government's might.

No beam. Maybe the Federation sent this one. Connell narrowed his eyes and spat on the ground. Damned Federation.

He checked the horizon. Nighttime would soon be upon them, and the twin moons would bring the tides. He must act quickly to save the man/machine/whatever that had just blown the pod to the mountains. A deserter then, who didn't want to be tracked, and fast enough to do the deed before the Federation found him. Interesting. And potentially deadly. A criminal, maybe? No, the Federation would have detonated any prisoner the moment they escaped bounds. Connell shuddered at the memory of how he knew that fact, when a man he'd spent an evening with turned out to be a rebel.

With no use for the Federation, which made huge demands in exchange for protection, supplies, and additional colonists which never came, Connell wasn't alone in despising the self-proclaimed rulers of the universe. Rulers who demanded the better part of their crops while robbing them of the young people who were needed to help with the harvest—presumably to make more bio-engineered soldiers. Oh, well. The soldier currently in the path of high tide had been someone's son, once. Far be it from Connell not to offer assistance—providing this wasn't a Federation trap. While he had reason to hate the Federation and all it stood for, he couldn't leave someone to die in the oncoming surf. Precious life wasn't to be taken for granted, as he'd learned when the man he'd slept with vanished before his very eyes. There one minute, gone the next. No warning. No time to cry out. Just... gone. How many more had the Federation claimed in a similar manner?

He'd made his way halfway across the sand with his sled when he heard the first wails. Cold chills raced up his spine. A terror? Hunting in broad daylight? One of the huge beasts he might hold off, but not a whole pack, and they seldom traveled alone. Roughly the size of two men when fully grown, the voracious carnivores feared nothing. The sound came again, more familiar this time. Not a terror, but the screeching protests of a small child.

A baby? The soldier carried a baby? More cautiously now, fairly certain of a trap, Connell approached the still figure. The crying grew louder and more aggrieved.

A handsome face stared up from behind the duro-glass of the soldier's face shield. The man blinked, but otherwise remained quiet.

# The Sentinel

"I am Connell," Connell said. Was the thing hurt?

After a long moment the mixture of man and machine replied, "I am Fort'een, and yours to command, Colonel."

Fort'een? What kind of name was Fort'een for a humanoid? The soldier's crystal blue eyes slid shut. Was he dead? Asleep? In stasis while his biomechanical suit repaired damage? Connell had heard of such marvels in recruitment ads, had read of their ilk before he'd left civilized worlds for a backwater colony and a new start. But how to fix a broken one he hadn't a clue.

With a bit of maneuvering he managed to arrange his foundling on the sled on top of the day's catch of fish. Howling emerged from inside the thing's breastplate. Connell ran his hands over the soldier's exoskeleton suit. There had to be a latch, right? How in the world did the soldier get the thing on or off? The moment he touched the man's helmet a mild shock coursed up his arm. Ow! "Okay, okay, I'll leave him alone," Connell grumbled.

Warily eyeing the helmet, Connell strapped the soldier with his screaming burden to the sled and slipped into the harness. In the distance the waves roared, and he checked the sun once more. Time to get moving. Now! His leg muscles burned and he hunkered low, grunting as he dragged the heavy transport across the sand.

The first of the waves rumbled across the vast shore as Connell reached the cliffs and clipped the sled into place. Hand over hand he worked the pulleys to raise himself and his cargo. Salty spray rained down on him. The village might be disappointed that he'd brought few fish home this evening, and the elders might condemn him for the soldier, but several couples with quiet dwellings would battle for the child—so few were born these days, and what ones survived infancy were carted off by the Federation.

Connell wouldn't think of injustice now. He'd apply himself to getting the strangers to safety. He could always wait to visit the village later. The wailing stopped about halfway up, and he employed the local tradition of praying to the twin moons that the infant merely slept. It took longer than normal to reach his home, what with hauling three times the weight of the heaviest harvest he'd ever taken in.

His stone cottage shone like a beacon in the fading light of the sun, and the twin moons rose over the bay along with the evening wind by the time he'd stored his catch and wrestled his unexpected guests into his home. He chopped herbs and diced roots to add to a simple fish stew, and while dinner simmered he knelt down next to the stranger again. His tentative touch to the breastplate cracked open the hull. Connell gasped and jumped back. How did that happen? Had he broken the suit? Would he get zapped again for his troubles?

The visor slowly lifted, revealing narrowed blue eyes. The soldier spoke, but his words were undecipherable. "I don't understand," Connell told him.

More garbled sound followed. Finally the man said, "Talk."

"About what?"

"Talk," the man repeated.

Connell helped the stranger remove portions of his suit, though the helmet remained in place.

*What the hell should I talk about? What does he want to hear?* "I know it's not much, but welcome to my home," Connell said, puttering around the room, lighting fish oil lamps to drive back the coming darkness. "The twin moons are in their final phase, so we're having a poor fish harvest. It'll pick up again when the weather clears."

The soldier stared impassively. Squirmy sensations wound around Connell's insides. "I came to New Wailea

## The Sentinel

six years ago," Connell prattled on. "I lived in the village until... until I decided I preferred my own company and found a way to get up and down to the beach to harvest fish." Liked his own company. Liked not hearing the villagers' murmured speculations behind his back painted a more accurate picture. "We're having fish stew for dinner. You do like fish, don't you?"

The soldier remained quiet, entire attention focused on Connell. The squirmy feelings intensified. Connell continued, "I lost my parents young and grew up in an orphanage on Tanaina 4."

When the man finally unstrapped a squirming child from his chest, both Connell and the man, Fort'een, rather, breathed heavy sighs. The child appeared grumpy and soiled, but otherwise unharmed.

The child began to cry and a pungent aroma filled the cottage. "I'll be right back!" Connell blurted. Looked like he'd visit the village tonight after all.

By the light of Shun and Nan he raced to the village, then returned, tugging on the arm of a scowling midwife. "You've been too long in the sun, Connell, when you imagine finding babes on the shore instead of stranded fish."

The unmistakable sound of an unhappy child split the night. "What are you waiting for?" exclaimed the midwife, grasping Connell's wrist in a claw-like hand and charging toward the cottage. She pushed open the door, and Connell barely had time to tackle her to the floor before the ozone odor of a particle weapon discharge seared his nose. He rolled upright, placing himself between the woman and his mysterious guest's outstretched hand.

Fort'een crouched in a corner, cradling the child. Fully dressed in his suit once more, he more resembled a metallic beast than a man. His weapon remained trained on Connell and the villager.

Oh shit! It suddenly occurred to Connell that bringing a Federation warrior home wasn't the smartest thing he'd ever done. The cybernetic being with the ability to end life in the blink of an eye homed his vision on the midwife. "Human female," he said, as though puzzling out some great mystery. "Advanced age."

Palms splayed, Connell held his position yet managed to capture the soldier's attention.

"Why here?" the armed threat asked.

"For the baby," Connell said.

The soldier cocked his head to the side. One big, mitted hand patted the squalling infant, tucked once more into the soldier's breastplate. "Mine." The soldier's fingertips remained rigidly pointing at Connell, and Connell stared at the small openings in the mitt. In different circumstances he'd have been fascinated by the weaponry. Now? Not dying at the hand of his house guest would be nice.

"She's here to care for the child," Connell tried again, a trembling sweep of his hand indicating a now furious baby.

The soldier glared and retreated further back into the corner. "Mine!" he growled again.

"Yes, yours," Connell agreed. "But the baby's clothing is soiled and it needs to be fed."

The soldier spared one glance for the child, one for Connell, and then nodded to the old woman peering out from behind the door. He spoke a few phrases in some strange tongue. Connell understood only two words: "Not hurt?"

Connell puzzled over the question. Was he asking if the midwife was okay or was he wondering whether the woman would hurt the child? The protective way he held the infant was all the answer Connell needed. "No, she'll not hurt the child, I promise."

# The Sentinel

After a few more moments the soldier rose and crossed the floor. Very gently he placed the child in the woman's hands. "Human. Female. Infant. Mine," he said.

Though the woman's eyes were wide and she gulped audibly, she took the baby. "In the morning. I'll bring her back in the morning." With a final nervous glance at Connell, she ducked out the door. Her footsteps hastened away.

Fort'een eyed Connell, standing at rigid attention. Then he sighed, or rather, issued a noise reminiscent of a sigh. After a moment, Connell realized the edges to the plates that pieced together to create the man's body armor had slid apart with a hiss. Section by section the soldier dismantled his covering. First he removed the breastplate, revealing a powerfully built chest totally devoid of hair. Next came the sleeves. A discreet glance inside that Connell hadn't managed earlier revealed sensors and other marvels he'd only seen once before — in the ship that had brought the original colonists to New Wailea. An impressive display of muscles relaxed and contracted as Fort'een continued removing his armor. Bulging leg muscles came into view next, and Connell blushed when the soldier unclipped that portion of whatever material turned him from man into fighting machine. He was totally nude underneath the suit so far. The girdle joined the rest of the suit, and a dozen or so devices that might have been weapons, in an organized pile. Beneath the marvel of science the soldier wore a pair of thin pants that unrolled to cover him from waist to ankles. A sigh of relief escaped Connell, even while a niggling of disappointment filled him. What he'd taken in of the gorgeously arranged warrior was enough to whet Connell's appetite to see the unrevealed bits.

*Stop thinking like that! What if he's like the villagers and prone to cast judgment?* What would the soldier do if he knew what thoughts chased themselves around his host's brain? Connell turned away, lest his appreciation for the stranger's form be noticed.

Fort'een pointed at his helmeted head. "Translator," he said. "Can't understand without." His words were clipped and emerged in an unfamiliar cadence, like he seldom spoke, or was unused to human language.

Connell nodded. Fort'een pressed a series of buttons from beneath a concealed panel on his visor. Odd clicks and hissing followed. Finally, the helmet slowly rose, Fort'een's large hands lifting it from his head.

The moment the apparatus cleared, Connell's heart stuttered in his chest. He froze in place, stunned by the sheer beauty of the being standing before him. Taller than the average colonist of New Wailea, the man stood six four or better, his larger frame necessary to carry the bulk of the suit, no doubt. Bright blue eyes gazed out from a face that seemed chiseled from the stone that village women used to fashion plates and bowls. A well-formed nose and sharply defined cheekbones topped full lips and a deeply cleft chin. Fort'een's close-cropped hair nearly matched the honey-colored wood of Connell's table, chairs, and bed.

Oh! Bed! Since Connell had inadvertently invited the stranger to stay, where would the man sleep? And would he wake from a bad dream, see Connell as enemy, and kill, as soldiers existed to do? There was the fish cave, where Connell stored his harvests, a smelly, cold place, chilled by sea water from underground. No, Connell could never send someone there.

*Sniff.* Was something burning? The stew! He rushed to the area set up for cooking and fumbled for a spoon to stir their forgotten dinner. Scorched maybe, but not burned, thank the twin moons. His tiny table boasted two chairs—one seldom occupied by a dinner guest. He ladled up two bowls of stew and placed them on the wooden surface. A quick trip to the well added water for them to drink.

Throughout dinner preparations Fort'een merely stood at the edges of the kitchen, observing, as though cataloguing Connell's every movement. Connell's, "Sit, eat," earned him a quizzical, raised brow gaze. "Food," Connell tried again, spooning up a taste of stew and moaning unnecessarily loudly when the liquid touched his tongue.

The soldier's eyes widened but he didn't sit. "Suit," he said, in his broken speech pattern. "Gives needs."

His suit? Perhaps he simply didn't trust Connell enough to accept a meal. Most colonists reviled Federation soldiers, and once more Connell questioned his judgment in bringing this one to his home instead of letting fate decide the man's future. In the distance waves smacked against the cliffs, high tide having arrived in force. The soldier would most certainly be dead by now if not for Connell's intervention. And the baby. A smile tugged up the corner of Connell's mouth. The tenderness in the big man's eyes whenever they'd fallen on the child must prove him capable of more than killing, right?

Fort'een folded himself onto the floor, watching each movement as Connell ate. Unease settled over Connell at being observed during the simple act of having dinner. Whenever his heart began pounding in fear, he imagined the soldier with the baby and his fears calmed somewhat.

After cleaning the dishes, sponging himself off, and settling down for the night, Connell opened the window shutters to let in the air. While the villagers feared living so close to the sea, Connell welcomed the crisp and salty scent of the ocean breeze, the proximity to the fish whereby he made his living, and also the isolation from the others.

Now, however, he faced a problem. What should he do with the soldier? "I..." Connell began, though not really sure what he'd say.

Fort'een solved the problem for him. "I stand watch." With surprising agility he redonned his suit. After a last, long look at Connell, the stranger wandered away into the night. Where was he going? There! The twin moons reflected off the soldier's armor where he sat on the cliff, staring out to sea. Didn't he sleep? Or was he asleep?

Several times in the night Connell rose to check out his window, and each time found Fort'een motionless on the rocks. At last sleep claimed him. *Would that he not kill me before dawn breaks.*

He tossed and turned, and woke with a start when his dreams of exploring the nooks and crannies of the soldier's muscles ended with a pool of seed on his belly.


Connell awoke to find Fort'een pacing the cottage, wearing the long, gray pants and his helmet. The moment Connell's eyes popped open the man demanded, "Is morning! Where is child?"

As if in answer, a rap sounded against the door. Before Connell could issue a warning, the soldier stalked across the floor and threw the wooden panel wide. There stood the midwife, baby in arms and a pack on her back. Ignoring the stranger's scowl, she stepped into the cottage. Connell couldn't help noticing her assessing gaze and small nod of approval at the soldier's toned physique. "I have everything you need for the day," she said. "Do you know how to change a baby?"

"Change into what?" Fort'een asked.

The woman smiled and promptly crossed to the table to demonstrate. Connell took advantage of

# The Sentinel

their distraction to pull his pants beneath the covers and remedy his nakedness. When he glanced up he registered a small flinch from Fort'een and would have laughed at the soldier's horrified expression as the man realized what the midwife intended. Taking pity, Connell hurried to the table and took a turn changing the cooing baby. Though an orphan, sent to New Wailea to make his fate, before he'd left the Federation worlds he'd helped plenty in caring for infants left parentless by conflicts within the galaxies. Some had required a whole lot more specialized care than a human child. Morphians! Yikes! Try changing a child who not only fought with two arms and two legs, but sixteen tentacles! And a nasty attitude.

The little girl gurgled and smiled, and... the soldier smiled back. The rigidity of his hardened features softened when he stared at the child, and when the baby wrapped tiny fingers around his larger digit, the sheer amazement on the man's face melted Connell's heart. This man was a killer? He seemed no more a remorseless machine capable of decimating worlds than Connell was himself—and the military had formally announced Connell incapable on his eighteenth birthday, due to not meeting their size requirements.

"Here is what you feed her," the woman said, producing a device Connell had seen many times before to deliver nutrients to a child too young to eat solid food.

"I've taken care of children before," Connell told her.

She nodded. "Then I'll be back this evening to collect her."

The sudden stiffening of the soldier's shoulders announced his understanding of her words. "Mine," he said.

"Yes," replied the woman, "but would you rather get up every two hours at night, then have to work all day, when it's my responsibility to care for youngsters?"

Before the stranger could answer, Connell replied, "We thank you for your help."

The woman left and warmth once more returned to the room with the stranger's smile.

# CHAPTER THREE

Fourteen wore the child carrier on his back as he'd done for the past few days, an improvised canopy shielding the baby from the bright sun while they worked. Several village women repeatedly offered to keep the child while he helped his colonel harvest the flopping silver bodies left behind by receding tides. But the child was his to care for, though Midwife insisted on taking her every night. The women of the colony wanted Fourteen, he knew, for his suit detected their arousal. He didn't want the women, and their constant giggling and tittering confused his language translator, his suit proclaiming the grating sounds as Old Trevorvian—a language long dead. Colonel? Colonel worked quietly, unless ordered to speak to allow the suit time to gather words, and his talk was slow and even. Soothing. It wasn't mind to mind, but... pleasant. How Fourteen would love to connect with his colonel's mind. So much more efficient than cumbersome words.

His suit also picked up arousal from his host, arousal that disappeared when the women arrived. Hmm... Worth further study. And while his host wasn't quite as large as most of the soldiers Fourteen had lain with, he was appealing and humanoid.

And the more time Fourteen spent without the neuro-inhibitors or his suit, the more his arousal grew. By day he stripped down to his thin undergarment, only keeping his helmet on for translations, as Colonel seemed wary of body armor. At night Fourteen kept watch, fully geared, to allow his suit time to cleanse his body of toxins, feed him, and erase the day's exertions. Perhaps he should order it to care for his other needs as well, without fellow soldiers around to ease him.

Throughout each night since arriving he'd watched for enemies and listened for signals. Had he truly escaped? Would approaching ships detect his presence? He dared not destroy his suit, if such a thing were even possible. But—he smiled at his latest discovery—the world he'd landed on boasted an extreme amount of sunlight. His light-powered suit thrived on the abundant energy, and fish blasted into fine powder made a workable replacement for the minerals the suit needed, far superior to the synthesized chemicals supplied by the Federation. And while he and his colonel worked to harvest the stranded fish from the sands each day, each night Fourteen and his suit quietly worked in tandem, refining protocols to accommodate new circumstances.

Where once he'd studied battle tactics, now he searched the suit's database for tide and weather patterns. If only the programming contained information on child rearing. He gazed at the poor unfortunate life forms left behind by receding tides, leaving miles of damp sand until the return of the waves at nightfall. Some things he'd just have to figure out on his own, with Colonel's help.

The child squirmed on his back, releasing a few snivels that heralded a full-blown howl. He knew the drill. He smiled and held out a hand, telling his commanding officer to stop the sled. With careful hands he placed the child on the sled and changed her soiled clothing. Then he sat on the edge and held her in his arms as she sucked greedily at a bottle. Warmth he'd not experienced in a long, long time flooded through

## The Sentinel

him, and he couldn't help the smile that pulled at his lips. Though he'd been administered chemicals from an early age to enhance his body and fit him for duty, he'd never felt as powerful as when he held the girl in his arms. She needed him. She smiled at him. She gave him purpose over and above killing. And in the mindless task of gathering fish, in the company of a child and a gentle man, he found peace for the first time in his troubled life.

"What word used, people belong together?" he asked. Words. Such awkward things.

His colonel crouched down beside him, brushing careful fingers over the light golden fuzz on the baby's head. "There's many," Colonel replied.

"People who," Fourteen stopped, sifting through his hood's neurons for the proper term. "Care. People care, protect," he finally said with the help of his translator. How he longed to simply connect with Colonel mind to mind. So much easier, so much more efficient.

"Ah!" The colonel's teeth emerged from behind his lips in a gesture that suddenly made the day warmer. "You mean family."

"Family?" Not the right word. Fourteen had had a family once. They didn't care. They'd sold him for favor.

"Yes, family," Colonel said. "They care for each other, would do anything for each other." He placed his lips close to the sensor intake on the helmet, dropping his voice to a whisper. "Would die for each other."

"Would die," Fourteen repeated. Yes, he'd die for the child, as he would for his colonel.

"We can't keep calling her 'child' or 'baby'," Colonel said with a toss of his head toward the contented bundle of infant in Fourteen's lap. "We need a name for her."

If she were a soldier, she'd have a number, subject to change with assignment. With his campaign as "Fourteen" over, should he be 'One' now? Would that make the child 'Two'? And Colonel outranked him, so Colonel should do the naming.

"You. Name her?" Fourteen asked.

Colonel whipped his head up and stared at Fourteen with shock in his eyes. "Me? Me name her?"

"Yes," Fourteen replied.

"Well—" Colonel's expression took on the intensity it normally did when he was thinking. "I've always been fond of the name Pearl."

"Pea-rl." Fourteen tried out the name, how it flowed from his tongue. While speaking mind to mind was faster, words fascinated him, how to form them, how to speak them, how others responded. Still, the loss of a constant influx of thoughts and ideas left him... isolated. Could he somehow modify his helmet to allow him to instantly share ideas with Colonel? How about Pearl?

"Family," he said, testing the word with his tongue.

Colonel gave him a lopsided smile. "Family."

Once the baby, no... Pearl was fed and drowsing, Fourteen strapped her to his back and continued collecting fish to store in the cave. Every day he and Colonel filled the chilly space, and every morning they woke to an empty cave after villagers came in the evening, leaving behind vegetables, clothing, toys and pretties for Pearl—even a cradle—and other things they might need. Not a bad life.

A pity it could end with a single ship passing by. Would the colonists be punished for hiding him? Fourteen couldn't let that happen. "Family," he said again.

## CHAPTER FOUR

"Why do they do that?" Fort'een asked.

"Do what?" Connell responded, studying the young couple who'd just left the cave with a basket of fish. Pride surged through him that without the helmet on, Fort'een took great care to enunciate his words, though he still struggled at times.

"That thing with their..." Fort'een cocked his head to the side as though searching for a word. The wrinkling of this brow relaxed when he found it. "Lips. Why do they do that with their lips?"

Connell scratched his head, trying to decipher the soldier's meaning. Just then, the young man inclined his head and placed a kiss on his wife's lips. Then he bent and repeated the gesture on the cheek of his child.

"Oh! It's how people who care for each other show affection. When they part company, they'll kiss goodbye, greet each other with a kiss when they return. They also kiss when..." Connell let his words trail off, a flush creeping up his cheeks at what he'd nearly said. He fought back the image of Fort'een bending down and placing his full lips against Connell's...

Fort'een didn't seem to notice the broken off sentence, being far too busy watching the couple. "Kiss," he said. "Affection." He kept his eyes trained on the path until the family disappeared from view on the village trail.

Connell lay on his bed, the moonlight illuminating his housemate sitting outside on the cliff. Though the winds blew and the rains fell, Fort'een held his ground.

If Connell were a braver man, he'd march outside and insist upon Fort'een getting into the house this instant. Then he'd remove the armor piece by piece, dry the man with a soft cloth, and tuck him into bed. Into Connell's bed. Most of the women of the village probably entertained similar notions; but though many came daily, flocking around the unattached newcomer, the Federation soldier didn't respond to their advances, or their unspoken requests for him to expand the colony's gene pool.

No, the only female Fort'een cared about was Pearl, but sometimes, every now and then, Connell caught a curious gaze turned his way, particularly when he'd offered some kindness. And although Fort'een still found nourishment in his suit, he'd sampled Connell's cooking and had abandoned the suit's cleaning and shaving to bathe in the stream as Connell did. Was it wrong to sneak peeks at such a finely formed body?

And exactly what did the man want? He seemed happy to harvest fish, share Connell's unpretentious cottage, and care for the baby, but this man had seen all the Federation had to offer. He never spoke of the future, the past, or even much about the present, satisfied to simply listen, asking the occasional question. How long would he remain content in a place like New Wailea, with its violent tides, dwindling population, and primitive existence?

Sleep descended. Warm and cozy in his bed, Connell gave over waking thoughts to dreams wherein the man outside, shrouded in mist, offered to share the bed, and more.

*Bong, bong, bong!*

## The Sentinel

Connell shot upright. The village signal drum rang out again. *Bong, bong, bong!* An attack! Fort'een bolted through the door, eyes wide behind his face shield. "What is it?" he asked.

"Terrors," Connell replied. "Great beasts with sharp teeth and claws. But there's not been an attack in months."

"Human?"

"No. Vicious animals."

"Where?"

"The village," Connell replied, shimmying into his clothing. The creatures cared naught for fish, preferring animal—or human—flesh. He'd heard tales of the original colonists having nearly been decimated by the pack-hunting creatures.

Normally Fort'een avoided the village and the stares of the curious. Now Connell struggled to keep up with the man's long strides. Ignoring the rain, he slogged through ankle-deep mud, straight to the midwife's cottage. "Pearl?" he demanded.

"Safe," the woman said. "We're heading for the caves." She bundled the child up and darted out the door, followed by a youngster of perhaps six years and leading another by the hand.

A harsh breath wafted from the soldier's body armor. He turned to Connell. "Where are attackers?"

Connell led him to the north side of the village, the edge closest to the forest where the creatures lived. The Federation denied colonists proper weapons to defend themselves, fearing disgruntled settlers might turn any arsenals on their harsh masters, as had occurred in the past. Many a colony failed due to settlers' inability to protect themselves from indigenous life forms. Hiding in caves and defending themselves with arrows, slings, and farming tools was all the villagers could do.

"Go with others," Fort'een demanded. He raised the visor of his helmet, cradled the back of Connell's head in one massive mitt, and bent down to graze his lips along Connell's. "I'll be back." Fort'een's smile blazed like the noontime sun before he turned and disappeared into the night.

Connell stood on the path, fingers skating along his lips where Fort'een had kissed him. "He kissed me! Fort'een kissed me!" A roar split the night, followed by another and another. Though his heart went with his warrior, Connell's feet took him to the safety of the caves, where he picked up a spear and joined the other men who kept watch.

Throughout the night he strained his ears for news. A yelp, a roar cut short, the *zip, zip, zip,* of some kind of artillery. A streak of light from a laser weapon. Never had so large a pack descended from the higher elevations, and never had an attack gone on so long. Would the village have even survived without Fort'een's help? Outnumbered and alone, would Fort'een survive? Connell spared a glance behind him to ensure Pearl's safety, then whispered a prayer for his family, his heart warming even in the cool, rainy evening to discover that, unbeknownst to him, he, a cast-off soldier, and a child whose origins were still unknown had somehow formed the thing he'd always wanted most in the world. Granted, his family didn't quite match the villagers' notions, but it suited him just fine.

Towards dawn the roaring faded, the creatures moving farther away. Through early morning fog a lone figure approached. Even as Connell watched, Fort'een's amazing suit shifted and changed, bloody spatters disappearing, ripped fabric mending itself. Ignoring any possible reprimands from the others, Connell rushed forward. "Fort'een!" he cried. "Are you hurt?"

## The Sentinel

"My suit mends my body," the man replied, raising his visor to bestow another kiss. "How fare you and Pearl?"

The man had just saved an entire village of people, and only two of them mattered. Connell's heart swelled. "We're fine."

Fort'een looked past Connell to the midwife holding the baby. "Take her," he told Connell. "Let's go home."

Home. The word had never held much meaning for Connell. Now it meant everything.

They took the child and trudged back to their cottage, Connell uncaring that he and his—partner?— left behind a small fortune in terror pelts.

"Daughter," Connell said. "Daugh-ter."

"Daughter," Fort'een repeated.

"That's right." Connell pointed at Fort'een. "You father, Pearl daughter."

The vacant expression came over Fort'een's face that indicated he'd disappeared into his mind to communicate with his helmet. His eyes refocused after a minute. "What are you?"

*I am yours for the taking* sat poised on Connell's tongue, though he dared not say the words. The baby gurgled and waved her chubby legs and arms, distracting the man and saving Connell from having to answer.

*What am I, indeed?*

Once more, Connell lay awake. So many times he'd visited the garden alone to relieve tension. Did Fort'een have the same urges, and if so, how did he alleviate them, or did his miraculous suit tend those needs as well?

Outside the window Fort'een shuffled restlessly on his cliffside perch. Did the man get lonely sitting out there all by himself at night? Since he didn't sleep, maybe they should defy village custom and keep Pearl themselves at night.

A low moan carried on the breeze. What? Was Fort'een okay? Connell pulled on his pants and hurried to the cliff. "Is something wrong?"

Silence. After a long pause Fort'een whispered, "I miss..."

Connell had never considered that Fort'een might have left a lover behind. The moonlight washed over the man, his features vulnerable even while fully armored. Connell eased down beside the soldier. "I'm sorry. You loved someone?"

"Loved?" Confusion passed over Fort'een's face, gone a moment later. "Not loved. At night, I... soldiers... we." Even in the low light of the waning moons the man's blue eyes shone. He raised his visor. "We took comfort from each other," he finally said. "Suit is not the same."

"Oh?" Connell absorbed the meaning. "Oh!" His eyes locked with the soldier's. They moved as one, lips connecting. A gasp of surprise gave Connell his opening to dive his tongue inside Fort'een's mouth. Ever since he'd first arrived on New Wailea to discover the hard notions of the colonists, he'd despaired of ever experiencing the physical pleasures he'd found with other young men at the export station where he'd waited patiently for an immigration opening. He'd snapped up the first opportunity, overlooking the requirements and a carefully worded call for "breeding stock." Small colonies had little use for those not inclined to increase the genetic pool to prevent inbreeding.

Fort'een drew back. "But I cannot ask that of my commander."

"Your... your what?" While the soldier's vocabulary skills had grown over time, he still missed the odd word on occasion.

## The Sentinel

"You are my commander, my colonel. I cannot..."

"Colonel?" Only then did Connell recognize the subtle inflection that wasn't "Connell" as he'd always believed, but "Colonel", a soldierly rank. He threw back his head and laughed. "I'm not your colonel, I'm a civi... civil..." Drat! Now words failed Connell.

"Civilian?" Fort'een offered.

"Yes, a civilian. Connell is my name, not a rank."

The soldier flashed a brief, barely perceptible smile and began to descend again. Connell stopped him. "Your name? Is it really Fort'een, or is that some kind of military name too?"

"Fourteen. My comrades were Thirteen, Fifteen, and Twenty-seven."

A number? All this time Connell had been calling the man by a number? "Don't you have a real name? A name given to you by your mother or father?"

Fourteen's lips drew into a thin line of distaste. "I would not speak of them. You have taught me what family is. They were not family."

"Then I will erase the bitterness from your mind." How many times had Connell dreamed of having a family while living in a Federation orphanage, a place too overrun to even hope for adoption? The very young, the beautiful, the exotic children found a place, but not someone like himself with no skills or looks to speak of. Fourteen, though, would have been taken in a minute, probably by an unscrupulous person who planned to raise him for use in a pleasure house.

This time, when Fourteen closed the gap between them, Connell opened his mouth. While hesitant at first, the soldier soon joined in the tongue play. Earlier he'd asked about kissing, yet he'd mentioned finding comfort with other men. Had none of them ever kissed him? Had they shared their bodies only?

"Come with me to my bed," Connell said. "We'll be more comfortable there." He rose and held out his hand. The soldier took it, and together they strolled the moonlit path to their home. They fell onto the bed in a tangle of arms, legs, armor, and heated embraces. Clicks and clanks announced the suit's plates hitting the floor. The helmet fell last.

Though the night hid details from Connell's eyes, he ran his hand up Fourteen's arms, seeking out the tiny depressions where suit gripped flesh, and where he knew tiny wires punctured muscles and drilled past tissue to arrive at the central nervous system, to add nutrients and take away toxins, to adjust the soldier's body for maximum efficiency, and otherwise alter his physiology for maximum performance and longevity. Ah yes, watching a living, breathing soldier had greatly advanced Connell's knowledge of how they worked.

In response to Connell's explorations, the soldier did his own discovering, dipping his fingers in the ridges of muscles on Connell's back and shoulders—muscles honed by pulling a sled full of fish across sand, and hoisting pulleys to raise the bounty up the cliff face.

"Family." That single word gusted from the soldier's mouth to Connell's ear, saying many things probably foreign to a warrior tongue.

"I want you," Connell murmured. "I've long wanted you, in my arms, in my bed, in my body." He rolled to the side, then onto his back, spreading his legs.

"I would have more kissing first." Fourteen climbed above him, sealing their mouths together once more.

The soldier's cock nestled against the cheeks of Connell's ass, bumping against his hole. Connell reached back and fondled the length and width. Already the anticipated burn to come sent tingles up inside. Oh, to be filled so completely by this man. But what could they use for lubrication? Spit? A bit of cooking oil? He reached under the bed for the small vial kept there, hoping the soldier wouldn't figure out exactly how Connell put the oil to use while alone in bed at night. He smeared the dampness against his hole, venturing a finger inside.

*Fuck me, fuck me, fuck me!* he silently chanted.

Though every bit as hard as Connell, Fourteen seemed in no hurry. Gentle kisses turned fierce, and hesitant groping emboldened, yet still Fourteen avoided direct contact with the places on Connell's body that might trigger release.

When at last the kiss broke, Fourteen skated his lips over Connell's eyelids, across both cheeks, and down to his neck. Connell moaned and Fourteen released a chuckle, the first laughter Connell had ever heard from the man.

With tongue and a gentle application of teeth, Fourteen mapped out the contours of Connell's neck, shoulders, and chest. Whereas Fourteen's body boasted little hair, a dark mat of short curls adorned Connell's own torso. Fourteen sifted his fingers through the mass while rising up for another kiss.

Finally (finally!), longer, thicker fingers joined Connell's at his entrance, skillfully working in the lubrication. Giving up their kiss with a sigh, Fourteen slid downward to take Connell's neglected cock into his mouth. Oh, by the moons! How glorious! A mouth on him, for the first time in ages. And not merely any mouth, but Fourteen's.

A mouth on him, fingers in him, Connell's consciousness fuzzed around the edges. Though kissing seemed new to his partner, pleasuring a man certainly was not. Fourteen took Connell to the very edge of ecstasy, held him there, then backed away. The pressure built inside. Just a little deeper, a bit longer... Damn! Fourteen stopped once more, his melodic chuckle soothing to Connell's frayed nerves. "Patience," the soldier ordered, then began the exquisite torture again.

The double sensation of mouth and fingers ended abruptly, and Connell released a whimper of frustration. Fourteen's mouth covered his anew, the taste of his own pre-come sending a spike of desire straight to his groin. He fought not to come, but... oh, a thigh brushed against his straining flesh. Connell bucked up, sending his cock sliding against Fourteen. Fourteen shifted, bringing their erections in contact.

"No more teasing!" Connell opened his legs wider in invitation. He wanted, oh, did he want—the burn, the stretching, the filling...

A moment later, something larger than fingers breached his opening.

Slowly, slowly, Fourteen sank inside of him. Their bodies sealed together, then drew apart, breathy sighs mixing with harsh pants and the roar of the sea against the cliffs. Connell moaned when the length of his lover pushed inside, filling him so very completely. Fourteen's mouth roamed freely on Connell's neck and face, in constant motion. Weight braced on one arm, the soldier caressed Connell's skin with his free hand.

Time after time the man returned to Connell's mouth, as though having now discovered the joys of two mouths joined, he couldn't get enough.

Muscles Connell knew to be genetically altered bunched beneath his fingertips, and he scrabbled for purchase on sweat-slicked, marble surfaces. His hands came to rest on a firm backside that plunged and retreated like the tide, filling his body on the forward strokes and leaving him longing and bereft on the aft.

Gradually they fell into a rhythm, moving together as though two parts of a whole, designed to work in unison. In, out, the gentle swaying of their bodies yielded to harder thrusts. Outside, lightning crackled and rain beat against the roof, the weather keeping time with the intensity of their loving.

With increasing force Fourteen shoved into him, and Connell met and matched each stroke. Twin strangled cries announced their arrival at a mutual destination, and they lay in each other's arms, catching their breath.

Two heartbeats, thudding furiously. Deep breaths sounding in harmony. Gradually both slowed, and the storm moved farther inland. Nestled snug in the bed, Connell dared to ask, "Where are you from?"

Fourteen hesitated so long that Connell thought he'd either offended the man with the asking or that his companion had fallen asleep. Finally, a throaty, "From D391," reached his ears.

"D391?"

"Civilians call it Noorvik."

"Noorvik?" Really? Only the elite of the races resided on the Federation home world. The residents there weren't bound by colony law to hand over crops or children. "How did you wind up a soldier?" he blurted, only realizing his rudeness once the words left his mouth. "I'm sorry; you don't have to answer that." If Connell had only been a little bigger, he himself might have wound up with implants and weapons at his fingertips.

"I do not mind," Fourteen stated, in his oddly-inflected accent. "My father sought favor with the senators. When allowing them to use me for their purposes didn't win what he sought, he took more permanent measures." No anger, merely mild acceptance.

"Use you!" Connell rose up on his arm to stare down at the man beside him—likely bred to be the epitome of Federation beauty, to be used as a bargaining tool. He'd heard tell of such, had seen similar things in the facilities he'd called home. Some young men never recovered from their ordeals, their minds destined to forever wander in the past.

"It is nothing," Fourteen replied with some conviction. "I have family now. I have purpose. I no longer serve a corrupt Federation."

Connell tightened his grip on Fourteen's arm, willing the man to know the truth in those words. "Is there something I can call you besides Fourteen? Having a number for a name seems so impersonal."

The soldier's eyes glittered in the dark, and he held Connell's gaze a long moment. "What would you like to call me?"

"Did you ever have a name?"

Fourteen's words emerged on a growl. "I will not use the name they gave me."

Immediately Connell wished he'd remained silent, and hadn't reminded the poor man of times best forgotten.

More quietly, Fourteen said, "There was a boy, a... friend I believe is the word, who I met when I first entered the Federation camp."

A lover, maybe? Connell's heart constricted. What? Jealousy? "Were you close?"

A head shake said no. "He was... kind. No one had been kind to me before."

*I'm a lowly fish harvester, but what I wouldn't give to borrow that miraculous suit and lay waste to any who'd hurt this gentle warrior.* Connell damped down his indignation. "What happened to him?"

"He was too kind, others took advantage. He took his life." Was that a glimmer in those blue eyes? "I should have been kind in return. I was not. He died. I would be called by his name, to let him live again in some small way."

"What was his name?"

"Stone."

"Alright, Stone." Connell tried the name out for good measure. It suited his new companion—solid and unmoving. "Now, what..."

Stone stopped the questions with more kisses.

Connell fell asleep to the sensation of lips upon his face and awoke to find himself still lying in a secure embrace.

They packed up all they'd need for their day and waited for Pearl's arrival. Stone dressed in pants and boots and nothing else. His suit lay on top of their sled, collecting solar rays. Weeks spent in the sun lent his skin a golden hue, still much lighter than the mahogany tones of Connell's own skin. "Why does Pearl stay away at night?" Stone asked. "I need no sleep. I could care for her."

"It's tradition here," Connell explained. "One room cottages don't offer much space for intimacy, so children are kept by the midwife to encourage the birthing of more children."

"Intimacy." Stone rolled the word around in his mouth before letting it fall from his tongue.

"Intimacy. Ummm... what we did last night." Heat rose up Connell's face to his ears.

"Ah, intimacy." A little half-smile lit the soldier's face. "I like intimacy."

Oh my! He didn't just say that! Connell choked, fighting for and not finding words to answer what sounded like a delightful challenge. Any response died on his tongue when the midwife approached, surrounded by villagers, but without Pearl.

Connell raced up to her. "Where's Pearl? Is she all right?"

The woman shot a wary glance at Stone, then another at the magistrate, who'd come wearing formal robes. Not a friendly visit, then. "This couple have no children and have agreed to take the baby as their own."

What? "Now wait a darn minute! Pearl is ours, and she's not going anywhere."

The magistrate cleared his throat. "The child needs two parents, and this couple…"

"Stone! They're trying to take Pearl!" Connell shouted.

Stone made not a sound. He merely donned his armor, methodically snapping the pieces into place until he stood before them, no longer a man, but a human/machine hybrid, and a deadly one at that. He raised his hand. Two blasts pulsed from whatever weapon he'd invoked. A boulder shattered nearby, debris spraying the nearby bushes. The couple, the magistrate, and the midwife all jumped. Hell, even Connell couldn't help a wince. Over the past few weeks he'd grown so accustomed to Stone's tender side that he'd forgotten the man was a professional killer.

The magistrate recovered himself, for the most part. A shaking in his hands betrayed his true fear. "You'd use your strength against us?"

Stone calmly raised his visor. "I'll use my strength to protect my family, as I used it to protect your village."

"Family? Family!" the man sputtered. "Two men cannot be a family."

"Two men and Pearl," Stone corrected. He took aim at another boulder. It exploded into chunks.

"What was that for?" the magistrate asked, once he'd recovered from the shock of the blast.

"I need smaller rocks," Stone replied, "to add a room to the cottage for our daughter." To the midwife he said, very deliberately, "She sleeps here now. Go get my daughter. If I must come collect her…"

The woman fled, the magistrate on her heels. Only then did Connell notice that the couple who'd wanted

Pearl were no longer there. Smart people.

"Family," Stone said, before swooping down to kiss Connell.


Stone. Much better than Fourteen. Neural inputs zinged along his skin. Ah... his suit agreed. He sat on the cliff, staring out at sea, tuning his ears to hear if Pearl cried or his mate needed him. Mate. Some of the soldiers in his unit formed semi-permanent bonds, ended by death or reassignment. Stone had fought the temptation to get close, knowing any warm feelings couldn't last. The military encouraged short-term attachments; it kept soldiers content, and no one fought as hard as a soldier fighting to protect another. Like he'd fought for Pearl and Connell that day. And would again if threat ever came.

But today he'd experienced a strange sensation, one he'd not encountered before. The chemicals fed nightly into his body prevented sickness and slowed aging, but did being away from the ship counteract the meds? *Diagnostic*, he ordered. Numbers and symbols zipped past his peripherals. Nothing out of the ordinary. And yet today...

A magistrate, the midwife, trying to take Pearl. *Zip, zip, zip.* Point by point his blood pressure rose, until the suit administered an antidote. Instant calm slowed his pounding heart. Next he pictured Pearl when she'd returned, how she'd laughed and tugged at his visor. No matter how big and scary he might look in his uniform, the baby saw past that, saw past the machine to the man. As Connell did. Connell. And there it was, the twisting of his heart, the lurching of his stomach, the pressure in his chest. *Diagnostic*! he ordered again.

More numbers, more symbols, all meaningless. *What is wrong with me?*

*Readings are normal for extreme human emotion.*
*What emotion?*
The suit paused before offering, *Affection.*
No. He'd held affection for Connell and Pearl before. This was something above and beyond affection. *What is more than affection?*
*Love.*
Love? He'd heard of that. Two soldiers had cared deeply for each other. So deeply that they'd talked of deserting, going away to build a life together. The next day the commander came and took one away. The other wasn't the same after that, and soon died in battle. Stone swore he saw the man step directly into the path of that missile.

Now he understood. If anything happened to Connell and Pearl, he might seek out a missile of his own. Emotion! Emotion enabled those two soldiers to defy their programming, and emotion allowed him to rescue Pearl—the reason commanders separated those who grew too close, no doubt. He'd just have to ensure nothing happened to the ones he'd come to love.

He lay back in the darkness, staring up at a million glittering stars. Connell gave them beautiful names, like The Angel, and Shell, for a lovely twisted mollusk they'd found on the sand. Stone knew them as TR-749 and QL-9, gaseous balls around which other worlds orbited. How much had Connell seen of the universe? So many marvels Stone wanted to share with his lover. If only they could join minds as they did bodies, allowing Stone to share his memories, his hopes, his fears. To not be alone. How did humans survive, living with a lover but not fully connected to them?

*Lover. I have a lover.*

A bright light in the sky winked and moved. A ship. What would happen if any found him here? He'd have to make sure none ever did.

## The Sentinel

Closing his eyes, he brushed his consciousness against the ship's, ready to retreat at the first sign of threat. Unlike Stone's suit, which relied on his own brain for cognizance, the ship possessed a mind of its own, a necessary trait to maneuver a ship full of cryosleeping children from a colony to a Federation camp for training. Duty. A duty transport.

The colonists needed children to help populate this world more than the Federation needed additional soldiers to conquer alien races. Stone's lips curved upward. *Greetings and welcome,* he told the ship.

The Federation surely wouldn't miss one little vessel and fifty recruits, would it?

# CHAPTER FIVE

"Where is the ship that brought you?" Stone asked as he bounced his daughter on his knee. More and more visions of a wrathful Federation plagued his mind. He must act and protect the new joy he'd found. The cryoship that had made parents of nearly every joined pair in the village was merely a class-one drone vessel, not possessing the type of equipment required to ensure the planet's safety. Drastic measures were necessary. Never would Stone's colonel... his "Connell" or young Pearl be subject to an uncaring government's whims.

"I arrived by Federation transport," Connell replied. "It left after I disembarked."

"Is there a ship here? From before?"

"The Federation disabled it so the original colonists couldn't leave and renege on their duty agreements."

Considering the age, some parts might be worn or missing, but Stone doubted the Federation would hold much interest in the supplies he needed. "Does it remain, still?"

"Yes. Not far from here."

"Take me there."

Stone donned his full gear and hissed when the million tiny pinpricks entered his body, connecting him to his suit. Whereas once he'd felt naked without his armor, now the weight pressed down. Had he always seemed so awkward? And even with the peripheral reading telling him their temperature, general health, and their emotion when he touched Connell or Pearl with his mitts, he preferred what his fingertips revealed. The softness of their hair, the warmth of their skin, the bumps that rose when Stone ran a finger up Connell's neck. Without the armor he could pretend he was just a man, as any other in the village—until his needs drew him back to his suit. While Connell's cooking might sustain him for a time, he'd been altered too much to return completely to flesh.

He sighed. With all the circuitry throughout his body, and with the special nutrients fed to him by his gear, unless subjected to extreme battle conditions, Stone would exist long after Connell and Pearl departed the world. A heavy weight tugged at his heart. Having only just found family, giving them up was unconscionable. *Enough of that later, first to keep them safe.*

The ship had seen better days, and obviously hadn't been touched much since landing. Stone foraged through the narrow corridors until coming to the main flight deck. The beacon, that's what he needed, and the proximity warning to alert him to the arrival of ships in orbit.

He passed Pearl to Connell and hoisted his newfound treasures. "Take me to the highest peak."

The rest of the afternoon was spent arranging and testing the old equipment. He retrofitted solar panels for power, an abundant resource on a planet with plenty of sun to spare.

"What are you doing?" Connell asked.

"This," Stone held up a silver cylinder nearly his own height and plunged the end into the ground, "is a warning beacon. Any approaching ships will sound the alarm." He thanked the heavens for his translator hood, for he still hadn't mastered all the inflections of local language.

"And that?" Connell pointed at a square, boxy device.

"It is a liar."

"A liar?

"Yes. Ships approach a planet and send out a greeting, to see what creatures may live there. This device warns of high radiation, to drive away any who get too close." Simple, yes. Effective? Stone hoped so.

Connell rested his head on Stone's shoulder, cuddling a sleeping Pearl in his arms. Another funny feeling coursed through Stone, one his suit labeled "contentment."

"Why did the magistrate think that couple better than us?" he asked. They provided for themselves and their daughter quite well. And the village never lacked for fish.

Connell's shoulders lifted and dropped. "I guess because they're joined."

Stone glanced sharply at his mate. "We join. Whenever we can." In his opinion, they couldn't get Pearl's room built quickly enough, so they could join whenever she slept if they wanted to.

His enhanced night vision allowed Stone to observe the lovely flush to his Connell's skin, usually brought on by thoughts of mating. Stone loved mating. Even without voices in his head, when so close to Connell, the two became one.

"They say words," Connell said. "Then the magistrate pronounces them joined and they spend the rest of their lives together."

Rest of their lives. Sorrow tugged at Stone's heart. The rest of his life would far outstrip the rest of Connell's. "I would spend my life with you," he declared, for surely he would—if he could.

The baby sighed, joined by Connell. "And I with you. Before you came here, I attended my daily routine, but there was never a reason to get up, or hurry home, and nothing to look forward to."

"What words do the villagers speak when they join?"

"They differ."

There it was, that lovely flush again. "What is it?" Stone asked.

"It's nothing," Connell replied, too quickly to have been speaking the truth.

"It is not nothing. What are you thinking?"

Very softly, Connell whispered, "I used to dream of joining one day, of no longer being alone. I... I even came up with the words I wanted to use."

"Tell me."

"You'll think me silly."

"Perhaps." Stone kissed the tip of Connell's nose to remove any sting from the words. "Tell me anyway."

"My heart, my life, all that I am, I give to you, my mate. In laughter and in tears, forever to remain by your side."

The choked up feeling the suit called love lodged in Stone's throat, and for a moment, words wouldn't come.

Connell pulled away. "See? I told you you'd think me silly."

Words. Yes, sometimes inconvenient, sometimes confusing, but Connell's words? Melded minds never made Stone feel so close to anyone. He pulled his mate back to his side, dropping a kiss to Connell's mat of tightly-curled ebony strands. Only one way to prove it. "My heart, my life, all that I am," he replied, "I give to you, my mate. In laughter and in tears, forever to remain by your side." No matter what happened, he'd keep his word. And when Connell breathed his last? Well, Stone would just have to see if the abandoned ship held a laser cannon to step in front of.

After a moment, Connell repeated the vow, his voice hushed and reverent.

"What happens now?" Stone asked.

"Um... we're supposed to seal the deal by mating."

Stone discovered that fishing line and blankets made an excellent partition between Pearl's cradle and Connell's bed.

# CHAPTER SIX

"Come back here, you!" Stone dashed across the sand, chasing a giggling, four-year-old Pearl. Usually so serious, the big man's demeanor totally changed around the child who'd tied both of them around her finger. He still hadn't answered the question of a mother; whenever Connell asked, he merely shrugged and replied, "She's ours."

*Vrrrt, vrrrt, vrrrt!* Connell dropped the sled harness and stood stock still. That wasn't the terror warning; besides, the creatures had learned to stay away, thanks to Stone.

Stone snapped to attention. "The alarm! A ship's approaching orbit!" He raced forward with lightning speed, snatched up Pearl, and handed her over. "Make for the caves!"

The last Connell saw of his mate was the man in full armor, climbing the hill to the beacon.

"I have news," Stone said after he'd come to reclaim his family. "The Federation is revisiting duty laws. Some within the Federation itself complained about destroying colonies."

"About time if you ask me," Connell replied, "but how do you know?"

A rare, non-family generated smile dimpled Stone's cheeks. "The ship. An S-type cruiser, very intelligent. We spoke." He tapped his helmet with a fingertip.

Sometimes Connell forgot his mate came from another place. For four years he'd seemed happy here in the middle of nowhere. What would happen if he grew bored and wanted to return to civilization?"

"Stone?" Connell asked.

"Yes, Connell?" Stone stopped on the narrow track leading to their home. Pearl's legs dangled over his arms where she lay sleeping in his embrace.

"Do you ever think about leaving here?"

He answered by shifting Pearl to his shoulder and enclosing his family in a hug, kissing them both soundly on the cheek. "I cannot."

"Why not?"

"I belong here. With my family." All humor fled his face.

"Are you ready to tell me yet why you deserted?" Connell told himself he wouldn't ask, but the words slipped out before he could stop them. Whatever happened before lay in the past. Did he really want to know what atrocities Stone might have committed in carrying out the Federation's vengeance?

"Something happened," Stone replied, his voice as hard as his name. "I questioned all I'd been told."

"What was that, if you don't mind my asking?"

A pained look appeared in Stone's eyes. "I'd take back all my years of service if I could. Every life I took from a colonist, every village I laid waste to."

Connell's heart gave a painful lurch. He'd heard of entire colonies being wiped out by the Federation, but didn't want to imagine Stone, his dear, sweet Stone, carrying out such orders.

"I was wounded," Stone said, staring off into space. "My commander warned that cave crystals would block our communication, but I went in to find who'd shot me." He nodded toward the child in his arms. "I don't know who fired the shot that killed her mother, but the woman died protecting her child."

Moisture leaked from the corner of Stone's eye. Connell pretended not to notice.

"I needed to protect the young one, and I promised her dead mother that I would."

Connell squeezed underneath Stone's arms, giving his mate a hug. "Thank you for telling me."

"Do you think less of me?"

Children entered training camps to train day in and out for years, their systems flooded with chemicals to produce the perfect, obedient killing machines. And somehow, Stone managed to break his programming, abandon the only life he knew, for Pearl. "How could I think less of you, when you gave up all you knew to save our daughter?"

A brief flicker of a smile chased away the clouds on Stone's face. "I did, didn't I?"

"Yes, you did. As you've done every day since."

"Connell?"

"Yes?"

"Is this one of those times we should kiss?"

"Yes, Stone, I believe it is."


Stone shuffled from foot to foot, holding out his helmet. "I want to show you something. I've made modifications to my helmet. You'll never bond as I do, can't join your mind to mine, but maybe my present will work."

"Present?"

"Trust me."

Connell's breath caught in his throat when his mate lowered the heavy helmet onto his head. Tiny tendrils tickled the hairs on the back of his neck, turning into pinpricks. Oh, shit! They were burrowing into his head! Images flashed before his eyes. By the twin moons! What was happening?

Stone, the cottage, even Connell himself disappeared. Rain. Warm rain spattered skin much lighter than Connell's, though not as pale as Pearl's. Stone's? Was he in his lover's body? He glanced up, noticing the prism of colors in the spray. Not rain. Up and up his gaze traveled to the very top of a waterfall so tall the edges flirted with puffy blue clouds against a greenish sky. Where was he? He gazed down, catching glimpses of rainbow shapes flitting in the water beneath his feet, too beautiful to be the indigenous fish of New Wailea.

One moment he stood in a rainbow's spray, the next he sat on his bed, huddled in his mate's arms. "Where was I?" he asked.

"You saw?" Stone beamed, eyes sparkling.

"A waterfall. Bright fish. Green sky."

If possible, Stone grinned wider. "It worked. XI-47 is my favorite planet. I took leave there once and spent two days exploring." Leaning down put his lips so close to Connell's ear that puffs of breath caused shivers. "Did you enjoy your visit?"

"Yes! You loved that place and wanted to share it with me?"

"I want to share all with you." Stone kissed him. No matter how many years passed, or how long they stayed together, Stone never seemed to grow tired of kissing.


"Fathers?" Pearl stood in the doorway to the room they'd added for her, nibbling at her lip. A cascade of golden hair flowed down her back, and any who saw her blue eyes believed she was Stone's in truth, so marked was the resemblance. Age-wise, though, she appeared more sister than daughter to her father, who hadn't changed much since the day of his arrival.

Her dad, on the other hand... Just that day Connell had found more white in his hair, more laugh lines around his eyes. Not that he didn't deserve them. It seemed for the past fifteen years, since his mate and daughter's arrival, he done little else but smile. "Yes?" he prompted.

Pearl studied the floor, her white blonde lashes sweeping her cheeks. "You know Georges from the village."

"Yes. And?" A twitch appeared in Stone's cheek. They'd talked about this, the day their little girl would begin seeking a mate of her own, especially since she'd apprenticed to the weaver and spent much of her time in the village instead of under the watchful vigilance of her parents.

"And, I wanted to know if maybe he could come to dinner..."

Stone's jaw twitched harder. "Georges, you say." Living near so small a village greatly limited the possibilities, and although Stone and Connell both liked Georges, letting him tag along on fishing expeditions and allowing him to court Pearl were two different things entirely.

"That's a fine idea, Pearl," Connell offered, placing a hand he hoped would be calming on Stone's arm.

"A fine idea," Stone repeated, the twitch becoming a sinister grin. "In fact, I think we should dress up for the occasion."

"Oh, Dad! Father! Thank you so much!" Pearl dashed into her room, undoubtedly to change into the new frock she'd completed the week earlier and not noticing her father's scary mien.

"Stone." Connell added a warning growl to the name.

"What?" his mate replied with a look of faux innocence. "When he was little, Georges loved to look at my suit. Asked me a million questions. Surely he's still curious."

The silent sentinel stood guard, only, instead of sitting on the cliffs, Stone glared at the village path.

Connell watched out the window while he prepared a meal. What exactly did Stone plan? And should Connell try to stop him?

Finally, a familiar, lanky youth came trotting up the hill. *ZAP!* One of the few remaining boulders within viewing distance vaporized. Stone wrapped his still-smoking arm around a visibly shaking Georges—smoke Connell knew was for show, and a recent addition to the suit. He held his breath and heard his mate ask, "So, Georges, you will respect my daughter, right?"

After dinner, Georges' goodnight kiss on Pearl's cheek cost them another boulder.

Pearl and Georges stood in the clearing in front of the stone cottage she'd grown up in. It'd taken some doing, but Connell had managed to convince his mate not to wear "the suit" to the joining.

Two years. It'd been two years since Georges first made known his intentions; two years, and all remaining boulders within easy reach.

Never had Pearl looked so lovely. Was that a sniff? Connell shot a worried glance at his mate. "Something's in my eye," Stone said, rubbing a finger over his eyelid.

The young couple stood, surrounded by their families. "My heart, my life, all that I am, I give to you, my mate," their daughter said.

## The Sentinel

Even Connell choked up when the magistrate declared Pearl and Georges joined.

That night, instead of keeping watch on the cliffs, Stone sat lonely vigil in Pearl's now-empty room.

In the early hours of morning, Connell coaxed him into bed. "Remember the first time you took me, right here?" he asked.

"How could I forget?"

Gentle kisses grew more heated, and though well-acquainted with his mate's body, Connell explored anyway, taking his time as Stone had done that long-ago night.

When the sun rose he fell into an exhausted, sated sleep—in his lover's arms.

Connell studied his reflection in the stream, the lines around his eyes, the white taking over the darkness of his hair, and the eyes that didn't see as well as they used to. As he watched, a handsome man, unchanged by time, stepped up behind him, wrapped him in an embrace, and softly whispered, "I love you."

Shouts from the house of "Grandfathers! He hit me!" elicited sighs from them both.

"Let's get back up there before our grandchildren destroy the house," Connell said. They took their time walking the path, hand in hand.

"And you thought my suit destructive," Stone groused. "It could learn a thing or two from our grandsons."

"I could give up the suit," Stone argued for the hundredth time in fifty years. "Perhaps I'd age as you do."

"No," Connell replied, hand shaking a bit as he placed it on his mate's shoulder. "The village needs your protection. I'm merely grateful for the time we've had."

As if on cue, the ship warning sounded. Stone placed a kiss on Connell's forehead and headed out into the night to protect all he held dear.

# CHAPTER SEVEN

"Father, I'm afraid it's time." Pearl's snow white hair now matched her name. Stone nodded and enfolded his daughter into his embrace. Her tears dampened his collar. Holding tight to the child he'd abandoned his old life for, he closed his eyes and breathed in her scent. Home. Family. Love. Where once she'd depended on him for strength, now he relied on her. "What are we going to do without Dad?" she murmured, voicing Stone's thoughts. What indeed.

"I need to go to him." He blinked back tears and entered the room where his mate lay in the bed they'd shared. Old and fragile now, Connell bruised at the slightest touch, and many a night Stone stood watch in the house to keep an eye on his lover. And while he'd sat in the darkness, counting every inhale and exhale from the bed, he'd planned. Today would see those plans either succeed or fail. Stone swiped a hand against his damp cheek. No, failure couldn't happen. He wouldn't let it.

Too weak to fully raise his hand, Connell waggled his fingers. Stone dropped down beside the bed. "It pains me that you'll be all alone," Connell rasped. Without enhanced hearing Stone wouldn't have been able to hear the man.

He gave his mate a tight smile. "I won't be alone," he said, placing a kiss on his lover's head. Then he lifted his helmet.

"What?" Connell asked. Although he'd enjoyed seeing other worlds in Stone's memories, he'd never lost a touch of fear for the attire of a Federation soldier.

"I would give you a choice. You may leave here, and hope one day I can find you again, or you can join your mind with my mind, be a part of me, in truth, for as long as my body bears life."

"Is this possible?" Was that a tiny bit of hope shining in Connell's eyes?

"Remember the waterfall world? Trust me." Stone strapped the apparatus in place, prayed to the twin moons his alterations worked, and snapped the visor closed. "Is this what you want? You must decide." *Please say yes, please say yes.*

The steady whoosh of Connell's breathing sounded unnaturally loud from under the hood. Connell nodded, a mere dip of his chin, but agreement. Clinging tightly to his lover's hand, Stone waited. A warmth pressed against his back as Pearl joined him. She placed her hand on their joined ones.

Stone stared down at the three linked hands, two wrinkled with age, his relatively unchanged by the passage of time. The man he'd spent most of his life loving coughed, drawing Stone's attention upward. Their gazes met and locked. "I love you." Connell's lips formed the familiar pattern of the words, though no sound emerged from his dying body.

Stone witnessed the light leaving his mate's eyes. At his back Pearl sobbed, clutching at him with frantic hands. If she only knew what her father planned, but he'd dared not tell her. Not until he knew for sure...

Then Stone removed the helmet and placed it on his own head. Confusion, curiosity, a touch of panic.

Breathing out a sigh of relief, with his mind Stone said, *Hello, love.* Then he did something he'd always longed to do—wrapped his consciousness completely around his lover's, merging two minds into one.

*What? Where am I?* Instead of a feeble croak, Connell spoke with all the strength of the young man he'd been when Stone first found him.

*I harvested your consciousness. Now I'll never have to be alone, and neither will you.*

*But... but... how?*

*I was a soldier, not a scientist. Do you know how the tides work? No, and yet daily they drop their bounty on the sands and retreat again. Does it matter how it works? Wherever I go, you'll go with me. We'll be together, forever.*

Gradually the panic faded. *I'm still alive?*

"Yes, and will be as long as I am."

Connell peered out at the world through Stone's eyes, Stone's mind following along. "Oh, Pearl, don't cry!" Though he'd used Stone's vocal cords to craft the utterance, the words and will behind them were purely Connell's.

"Dad?" Now came their daughter's turn for confusion.

"I'm here, sweetheart. I'm with your father."

"How? No, never mind how! Oh, Dad..."

And once again Stone shared an embrace with his family.

*You know you have free access to my mind and memories now, right?* Stone asked.

*Really? You mean I could...*

*Yes.* Stone swallowed hard and led his mate through neural pathways, to the time he'd been fighting and had found a baby.


*I still don't understand how we're doing this,* Connell said, communicating mind to mind as Stone had once dreamed.

*Sometimes you don't have to understand something to appreciate it.* Stone knew all Connell needed was time before he'd come to accept their bond. Until he grew comfortable in his new circumstances, a little distraction might help. What wondrous places Stone could now show his love. *Come with me,* he said.

One minute they sat on the cliff overlooking the pounding surf, the next...

Warm droplets rained down, only now, Stone's memory added a younger Connell to the scene. Mouth against mouth, they tasted each other's tongues and the sweetness of the water falling upon them. In the shallows, the rainbow fish danced.

Stone laced their fingers together and led Connell to another marvel he'd discovered years ago, in another lifetime. On a bed of moss, softer than a whisper, Stone settled between his lover's spread legs. Connell raised his hands, turning them this way and that. "They don't shake," he said, awe in his tones. "They're not wrinkled!"

"You are as you were when we first met," Stone confirmed, before sealing their lips together. He'd shared his body with many a man, but never his tongue—or his heart. Those belonged to Connell only.

After delving into the wonders of Connell's mouth, Stone lowered his lips to firm pecs to sip the water caught in the dark curls on his mate's chest. The sweetness of the droplets and the muskiness of Connell's skin made an intoxicating mix. Lower and lower he roamed, until his mate's cock teased his lips. He opened, taking his lover inside. Stone tasted pre-come and honeyed water. Connell's balls drew to his body beneath Stone's fingertips.

"I want you," Connell exclaimed on a gasp. Stone maneuvered until his cock slid between Connell's lips. In their shared consciousness he experienced his own pleasure as well as Connell's. A swipe of his tongue up the underside of his mate's shaft sent chills zinging through them both.

He pulled out and once again positioned himself between the strong thighs he'd enjoyed for over half a century. A nudge at his lover's opening sent shockwaves directly to his groin, but also to Connell's. Through their connection, Stone enjoyed both.

Tight heat gripped him, while the glorious moment of entry teased his mind. Oh, fuck! He was fucking while being fucked. By the twin moons! And no need for cooking oil. "Do you feel me?" he asked.

"I feel you," Connell replied, wonder in his voice, "and yet I am you. Is this how I always make you feel when you're inside me?"

In answer, Stone kissed him, let the man feel the pressure in his chest, how he'd rather die himself than ever lose what he'd found on New Wailea so many years ago.

They rocked together, pressure from penetration vying with the sheer delight of plunging into a lover's body. Tension built, firing through Stone's groin and belly in double dose. Connell's gasp became his gasp, his moan emerged from Connell's throat.

Stone grasped Connell's hands, twining their fingers together. Skin to skin, mind to mind, inside and outside all at once. They fused and merged, the line between the two blurring, only to disappear in the pure white bliss of total completion. They cried out with a single voice.


*No.* Connell invoked a stern voice seldom heard during his life.

*Why not?* Stone challenged. It would be so easy. Connell's transition proved that.

*It wouldn't be right.*

*She'd still be with us!* Stone stared down at the bed where his little girl had once held her own little girl—now a grandmother of three herself. With each breath, Pearl faded more and more. A few seconds in the helmet and she'd live forever, exactly as she'd been the day they'd met, or at any point in her life she chose to remain.

Connell explained without spoken words. *We don't know where Georges' soul is but it's not in here with us. She'll find him. And I'm here with you.*

*But if she was a baby, sharing consciousness with her father and her dad, she wouldn't worry about a husband...* Oh. If Stone carried out his plans, he'd rob his daughter of the memories of her own family. He sniffed. *I can't stand to lose her.*

*We'll never lose her; she'll always be a part of us. We're her family.*

"Family," Stone repeated. "We're her family." He bent to kiss their daughter goodbye, then together, through Stone's eyes, he and his mate watched their sweet baby girl breathe out one final time.

They sat on the hilltop. The beacon pulsed, as it had been doing all day. "Just a cruiser," Stone assured his mate.

He stared up at the night sky. Did Georges now embrace Pearl once more, somewhere in creation?

His little girl was gone, taking his last reason for staying. His grandchildren all had mates, as did his great-grandchildren. With carefully selected ship landings over the years, he'd swelled the colony's numbers into the thousands—a colony still undiscovered by the Federation, thanks to the false warning he'd set up. Forty more villages dotted the planet surface, and in many, Pearl's legacy flourished. No, she wasn't really gone; she'd always live on in memory and through her descendants.

## The Sentinel

The cruiser approached hailing range. Nothing held Stone here anymore. *Have you ever been on a cruiser before?* he asked Connell.

*No, just a regular transport, sandwiched between excavation equipment and livestock.*

Stone grinned. *Want to hitch a ride?*

*Who'll stand watch here if we're gone?* Connell, ever the voice of reason.

*I'll set the beacon to alert us no matter where we are. Our body will still be here, waiting for the day we're needed.* Stone closed his eyes and focused on keying the beacon's frequency into the suit's receiver and setting up relays to bounce off passing ships. Tricky, but workable. The sleek little vessel nearing orbit hailed New Wailea. *Want some company?* Stone asked.

*Sure,* the sentient brain powering the craft replied.

*I'll show you the universe,* Stone promised his mate.

# EPILOGUE

"And that's the legend of the sentinel," the teacher said, snapping her book closed. Fifteen students stared in rapt attention at the statue before them of a man in an odd-looking uniform and helmet. Nels crept closer to glimpse through a clear face shield. Eyes closed, one side of his mouth quirked up in a half-smile, the man appeared so lifelike, so real, unlike most statues Nels had seen, carved of stone. When no one was looking he placed his hand on the statue's arm, only to jerk it back. Ow! That zap hurt!

Next to the statue sat two strange-looking objects their history books called "beacons". He'd looked up "beacons". Apparently they were some kind of warning device. Maybe touching them wasn't such a good idea. Nels shook his still-tingling fingers.

The teacher droned on about the heroic acts of the man named Stone. According to his great-grandmother, Nels himself had been descended from the great sentinel, though half the kids in his class boasted the same. Only, how could anyone be descended from a statue?

"Now, what's the sentinel's purpose?" the teacher asked.

Nels lifted his hand above his head. "He keeps watch over New Wailea, and if we're ever threatened, he'll wake up and keep us safe."

## The Sentinel

"Very good, Nels! Now..." the teacher stopped mid-sentence, eyes wide as she backed away.

*Vrrrt, vrrrt, vrrrt* split the air. "By the twin moons! What is that?" she gasped.

*Vrrrt, vrrrt, vrrrt.* The students screamed and scattered, the teacher chasing behind, shouting, "Wait! Wait!"

Nels froze in his tracks, staring fascinated at the statue. Did it... did it just move? He blinked hard. Then, as he watched, the face shield rose and one blue eye opened.

## THE END?

About the Author:

Somewhat of a nomad, Eden Winters has visited seven countries so far. Her earliest memories include making up stories for the family's pets, and through her academic years, she wrote many short stories and poems. Dreams of writing professionally were realized, only not as planned, with a good dozen years spent as a technical writer.

She began reading GLBT fiction as a way to better understand the issues faced by a dear friend and fell in love with the M/M romance genre. During a discussion of a favorite book, a fellow aficionado said, "We could do this, you know." Eden wrote her first novel shortly thereafter and never looked back.

Currently, Eden calls the southern US home, and many of her stories take place in the rural South. She lives alone, having successfully raised two children, and divides her time between a day job, friends, writing, trying different varieties of vegetarian cuisine, and outdoor adventures such as hiking and camping. Her musical tastes run from Ambient to Zydeco, and she's a firm believer that life is better with pets. She also loves cruising down the road on the back of a Harley Davidson.

Find Eden's other works at http://EdenWinters.com or contact her ar EdenWinters@gmail.com.

Other titles by Eden Winters:
- The Angel of Thirteenth Street
- Fallen Angel
- Settling the Score
- The Telling
- The Wish
- Duet
- Naked Tails

Other Rocky Ridge Press titles:
- From Eden Winters
  - Diversion (DIversion #1)
  - Collusion (Diversion #2)
  - Corruption (Diversion #3)
  - Manipulation (Diversion #4)
  - Redemption (Diversion #5, coming soon)
  - The Match Before Christmas
  - Fanning the Flames
  - A Lie I Can Live With
  - Summer Boys
  - Tinsel and Frost
- From P.D. Singer
  - Spokes
  - On Call: Dancing
  - On Call: Afternoon
  - On Call: Crossroads
  - Training Cats
  - Tail Slide
  - Donal *agus* Jimmy
- From Z. Allora
  - With Wings (Dark Angels #1)
  - Tied Together (Dark Angels #2)
  - Finally Fallen (Dark Angels #3)
  - Happy Holidays (Dark Angels #4)
- From Cari Z
  - Wanting More

Made in the USA
Lexington, KY
02 August 2015